Charles H Denison

Rhode Island

Charles H Denison

Rhode Island

ISBN/EAN: 9783337380076

Printed in Europe, USA, Canada, Australia, Japan

Cover: Foto ©Andreas Hilbeck / pixelio.de

More available books at **www.hansebooks.com**

A POEM

Delivered at the Annual Reunion

OF THE

Rhode Island Association of California,

AT FASSKING'S GARDENS, ALAMEDA,

October 7, 1876.

BY

CHARLES H. DENISON.

SAN FRANCISCO:

BACON & COMPANY, BOOK AND JOB PRINTERS.

1876.

ARGUMENT.

— ••• —

1. The name and productions of the State.

2. Building of the old Tower of Newport.

3. Banishment and Wanderings of Roger Williams.

4. The sufferings of the infant State tend to strengthen it.

5. The terrible " Narragansett Fight " at South Kingstown.

6. Ballad of the " Devil's Rock " in North Kingstown.

7. King Phillip retires to " Mount Hope," and dies by Treason.

8. Centennial Day, and the heroes of the Revolution.

9. The young Warwick blacksmith, who hammered Earl Cornwallis and received blows in return.

10. The Mansion House and story of a Shipwreck.

11. The good old Deacon and his treasure-trove.

12. Perry's Victory on Lake Erie, war of 1812.

13. The Sons of Rhode Island in the Civil War.

14. The City on the Bay.   Closing.

RHODE ISLAND.

There is a State whose southern bound
Infringes on Long Island Sound :
Where "Johnny Cakes" are legal tender,
Where six per cent. is paid the lender ;
Its islands white with frisking lambs,
Whose sand-banks discount long blue clams :
Its shores abounding with Quahaug,
Its waters swarming with Tautaug ;
Where maidens' cheeks, like roses red,
Are matched by boys on corn-cakes fed ;
This little State—you 've heard its fame—
RHODE ISLAND is its well known name.

1*

Before Columbus saw our land,

The Northmen touched its rocky strand : (1)

An indication of that hour

Is seen in Newport's lonely Tower,

Erected on Aquidneck Hill.

Irreverence calls it a " Mill,"

But ancient maps and records said

'T was built by Eirek, named " the Red" ;

And Dighton Rock inscription proves,

The Northmen there made warlike moves.

Perhaps they wintered in the Bay

And built this tower in which to pray

To their strange gods—no man can tell :

The ages keep the secret well.

'T was on a dreary winter's day,

A banished pilgrim groped his way,

Through blinding snow and stinging sleet,

With heart depressed with weary feet.

A persecuted, friendless man,

Escaping from religious ban,

Amid the savage wastes to plant

Religious freedom !   Far from haunt

Of men more stern than those from whom

He fled in days of England's gloom.

'T was sixteen hundred thirty-six,

The day of month we cannot fix, (2)

This man of nerve, unknown to fame,

Reached the bleak shore, from whence there came

A noble savage without fear,

Who spoke the welcome words, " WHAT CHEER !"

Each struggle of our infant State

You'll not expect me to relate ;

It had its time of deep depression,

Advancing now, now retrogression :

No State before had made its goal

The largest " Liberty of Soul !"

No State had laid such broad foundation

As this young " Providence Plantation !"

What! allow a man himself to think

What he should eat, or wear, or drink ?

What creed accept, what church attend?

Such latitude would never end

Until the men throughout the State

Would dare dispute the magistrate ! *

To check this daring innovation

Increasing fast in this " Plantation,"

Became the object and intent

To which each bigot's aid was lent.

The persecution quickly came—

As usual, in Christ's holy name—

As snow-flakes thrown against a rock,

Our State their puny efforts mock,

Until, like some young oak, which stood

Detached from all its brotherhood,

The more assailed by furious storm,

The sturdier grows its stately form ;

At length becomes a towering giant,

Unconquered, and yet more defiant,

Because its deepening roots take earth

Where freedom of the soil has birth.

* Cotton Mather's expression.

So on I pass, in proper order,

To tell of tales within our border,

Relating each important story

Of fact and fiction, war and glory.

Just forty years had passed away,

When, on another wintry day,

Battalions—led by men as brave

As ever filled a soldier's grave—

Through storm of sleet, through blinding snow,

Marched out to meet their savage foe,

Who, camped on island-fortress, wait

With rifle aimed by deadly hate,

With arrow and keen scalping knife,

To take their foremost foeman's life.

Yet onward press this daring band,

With banners and uplifted brand,

Until a swampy plain they reach (3)

Through which the stagnant waters leach ;

Then halt, and quick survey the ground,

Within South Kingstown's inner bound.

The sun was glistening on the plain,

The wintry sun was on the wane ;

Still struggling through the lessening storm

To send a cheerful ray to warm

The hearts that soon would be as still

And silent, as the snow-clad hill.

That brief survey, that glance around,

Gave information of the ground.

A broken tree with clinging moss

Was flung a stagnant ditch across ;

At best, precarious support

To firmer ground within the fort ;

A blockhouse on the inside stood,

With ports protected by the wood.

This narrow causeway all must face

To gain an entrance to the place.

A strong abbattis, chevaux-de-frise,

Made from the tops of fallen trees,

In width some more than fifteen feet,

Encircling until both ends meet

The island round ;—outside, a moat

So wide that eight canoes could float

Abreast, upon its sluggish tide

Before they touched the other side.

Inside the moat, huge tubs of grain,

Defended from the leaden rain,

Arranged in tiers, piled end on end,

The dwellings better to defend.

Behind this rampart, quiet lay,

Like tigers anxious for their prey,

The savage foes ; and silent wait

To consummate their deadly hate.

The wind had ceased, the snow lay still,

On meadow, and on far-off hill,

Concealing from all human sight,

With fleecy mantle, pure and white,

All faults and pit-falls of the land,

As waves make smooth the shifting sand.

The forest tops no longer bent,

Until by furious tempest rent ;

The feathery cloud upon the trees,

Unshaken by the whistling breeze,

Remained like peaceful banners white

That waved between the deadly fight,

While all unseen, hid deep below,

And silent yet, the lurking foe ;—

So broods the deathlike stillness o'er

The glassy sea, ere tempests roar ;

So serpents hide beneath the flower

To strike the traveler's fatal hour.

As waves when dashed upon a rock,

Are shattered by the dreadful shock,

With strength renewed again return,

Essaying still with effort stern,

To move the firm impediment

Until the earth-bound rock is rent —

So our brave men, that fatal day,

Essayed to pass that dread causeway ;

Three times from off its surface swept,

The enemy his fortress kept—

Six English captains death laid low,

That day, upon the crimson snow.

The warriors swarmed inside the pass,
Like hornets from their nest, en masse ;
Their yells resounded through the air,
As if a thousand fiends dwelt there,
And from their lairs within the place,
Might issue to destroy our race.

But *sound* alone could never swerve
From purpose stern those men of nerve.
Conclusions fierce they came to try,
And conquer there they would—or die.
The arrows whistled o'er the pass,
They issued from the dense morass,
And swept from island to the main,
Like shadowy clouds o'er summer's grain ;
So dark ! it seemed the storm once more
Might soon succeed the battle's roar.

The deadly rifle gave reply,
Its echoing voice ascending high,
Sometimes in volleys, oft alone,

Succeeded by an answering groan ;

Discordant voices now would die,

Then rise and fill the trembling sky,

Until, with thickening smoke and flame,

The place a very *hell* became.

While here in front the fight was waged

At other points it fiercely raged.

Brave *Moseley* found a way to float

His daring men across the moat,

And crawling through the deep stockade

Agreeable diversion made ;

Till soon the words, " They run ! they run !! "

Resounding, told the Fort was won,

And matted dwellings swept by fire

Became the red man's funeral pyre.

Our fallen Captains at this Fort

Were Johnson, Gallup, Davenport,

And Sieley, Marshall, Gardner ; all

Rested beneath death's sable pall.

Our total loss was *eighty-five*—
No INDIANS REMAINED ALIVE !

Of those not killed, some fled away
Before the ending of the fray,
Some sank beneath the stagnant. moat,
But most lay prone on wintry coat
Of snowy texture—battles done—
To bleach through wind, and rain, and sun.
Historians say—'t is sad to tell—
" A thousand Indians went to Hell ! "
From greater light we only say,
They bravely fought, that bloody day.
They strove for homes, laid down their lives,
To save their children, brethren, wives.
Like *that* melée, there's many a fight
Where both sides have a show of right.
Who die for Country, White or Red,
We number with the patriot dead :
White, Red, or Black, who die for others,
The *World* acknowledges as brothers :

New England or in Dixie's land,

We clasp with them the friendly hand.

———•———

Long years ago another scene

Transpired, not far from " Kingstown Green."

'T was when the old " Devonian Age "

Had written on earth's plastic page

Its foot-prints legible and plain,

With silt and sunshine, wind and rain,

Until it hardened into rock

That now withstands the Earthquake's shock.

I tell you of a bridal day,

That happened years ago, that way.

The maiden's choice was all too late

To save her from a queenly fate.

I cannot say this tale is true,

As told to me, I tell it you ;

Occur it did, in early day,

If not in *this*, some other way,

And if I mix the names and date,

Condemn it not, have patience,—wait,—

A poet has a right to say,

That *black* is white, that *blue* is *grey !*

Where the sparkling waters of the beautiful Bay *

Reflected the glances of the sun's bright ray

Not far from Apponaug, there dwelt a smart maid,

A belle of that day, modest, retiring and staid.

The house had a quiet and romantic air,

Although it was something in want of repair,

Embosomed in vines, by the side of the road

That led from the city and passed the abode ;

The roof was crowned high with a chimney of stone,

That seemed to be capable of standing alone,

'T was a fine country place, a sailor's snug berth,

And handy to travel from over the earth.

* In early records, the " Devil's Rock " in North Kingstown is mentioned as a boundary.

2*

One evening as Polly had set herself down,

By the wide opened door, dressed in her best gown,

Her hair a-la-mode, but not disarranged

To appear as though it had never been changed,

Nor flying about as the fashion is now

Concealing the most of a beautiful brow,

But dressed with good tallow, made from a sheep,

And combed in the place that she meant it to keep ;

No jewels she wore, but the sheen of her eye

Had the sparkle of glow-worms when evening is nigh,

And the rose on her cheek, with the tone of her voice,

Made Benedicts sorrow their own hasty choice.

She was six feet in height, her eyes they were blue,

And to tell you the truth, a little askew.—

I 've never yet mentioned her feet or her hand,

But the former, they said,—wanted plenty of land.

After all, she looked wholesome if not very gay,

Yet would not compare with the girls of our day.

As evening drew on, a Teamster came down

The hill near the house, just returning from town ;

He stopped his Ox team by Apponaug's daughter

And politely requested a drink of cold water.

He was covered with dust, was dressed in a smock,

That looked as in laundries he never took stock,

Notwithstanding all that he seemed a good fellow,

With complexion half way between blue and yellow,

So the girl hurried off to grant his request,

Her face wreathed in smiles, and she looking her best.

She quickly returned with a mug of sweet cider

Which caused him to open his eyes and mouth wider,

When down went the liquid in sweet gurgling tones :—

And the mug was as dry as the dust of the zones.

In an instant the form of a monster he took—*

The maid with affright and astonishment shook,

As she gazed at his face, her eyes full of tears,

His nose like the claw of a lobster appears,

A shock of thick eel-grass surrounded his head,

His beard of fine coral, a bright flaming red,

* This ballad is public property, and the story has been written before now, but in different language and metre.

His teeth like barnacles, that cling to a ship—
To which beauty now add a very thick lip,
And two clam-shells immense which served him for ears,
And you have the ensemble exciting her fears.

His resonant voice when he spoke was as loud,
As the thunder that rolls from the dark tempest cloud,
It threw down the chimney with a terrible crash
And broke several windows, including the sash.

" I'm King of the Bay," he said, " pretty maiden,
And I rule over all the Tautaug and Menhaden,
I'm tired, my dear girl, of a bachelor's life,
And have fully determined to make you my wife.
You shall rule all the eels and small-fry, and ride
On the back of a Dolphin, a beautiful bride,
While my subjects shall gaze with mouths opened wider,
Than mine when I drank up your mug of sweet cider.
Then he caught her while screaming with terror and fright,
And to North Kingstown brought her that very same night.
And there from a rock, with Apponaug's daughter,
He sprang with a yell beneath the blue water,

And the prints of his feet, as the wiseacres say,

Impressed in the rock, have remained to this day,

And her scream is still heard along the old beach

At twilight's lone hour, like the osprey's shrill screech.

Who disbelieve this tale, I say,

To Kingstown go, and see to-day

The self-same rock with foot-prints fair

As sculptor e'er could chisel there,

And sitting yet, by open door,

Much fairer maidens than of yore,

Who, patient, wait from day to day

The coming of the " King o' the Bay."

A postscript I will add, just here,

Or, rather whisper in the ear,

To bachelors of every Nation,

This most important information.

Rhode Island girls are housewives neat,

In Castle Hall, or Cottage sweet :

Familiar are their hands to make
A silken dress, or "johnny cake."

You 've seen the beauteous damask rose,
The lily, white as Alpine snows,
And both, when tinged by rising sun,
Their glories mingled into one?
Complexions of such white and red,
With golden halo o'er them shed,
Where e'er Rhode Island girls you find
These glorious beauties are combined.
Yet, not alone of blondes I sing,
Some tresses match the raven's wing.
As purest gems emit their spark
The best, when glittering from the dark,
So there are eyes whose flashing light
Would guide you through the darkest night.
And if by tempests you are cast
Upon their shores, and chilled by blast,
Their hearts and arms are strong to save,
Like Ida Lewis, *all* are brave !

I pass along from gay to grave,

To finish up my staggering stave ;—

Since " Kingstown Fight," historic made

By desperate valor there displayed,

Where dread Wampanoag's kingly son,

So quickly fled, when fight we won,

To Bristol's beauteous " Mount of Hope,"

Escaping when he could not cope

In numbers, or with weapons crude,

And deeply hid beneath the wood,

Until his blood by Treason's hand

Was spilled upon the shuddering land ;—

Had passed two hundred years away,

Which brings us to Centennial day,

In eighteen hundred seventy-six.

Midsummer's day our drink we mix,

To celebrate a freeman's right

To pay illegal tax, or fight.

Our Fathers chose to fight, and we

Enjoy their dear-bought liberty.

We glory in those men of yore,

Who drove the hirelings from our shore,

Who flung our banner to the breeze,

Who built our towns, uprooted trees,

And scattered wide the golden grain,

From Alabama, north to Maine ;

And formed for us this mighty Nation,

Fair Freedom's last and best creation

And now, to-day, with mother land

And nations all, we shake the hand.

But let me in brief terms relate,

Our Fathers' struggles for the State,

Beginning first at Lexington

Until at Yorktown they had won.

I ask you to remember still

The fierce attack at " Bunker Hill,"

Where Putnam fought, where Warren fell,

Where monumental tablets tell

Suceeding generations how

Those patriots fulfilled their vow,

And those who could not do the fighting

Put down their stern resolves in writing.

John Hancock made a heavy scrawl,

Like plain handwriting on the wall ;

Our Hopkins wrote a trembling hand,

Like insect straggling o'er the sand ;

The Adamses, and Roger Sherman

Cared nothing for King George, the German,

And Franklin, of the lightning hand,

Inscribed his name, and took his stand,

With Jefferson, and all the others ;

A most determined band of brothers.

I cannot call their names all here,

On sacred Roll they now appear,

And he who runs may see them there.

As plain as lightning scroll in air.

Those stern resolves, so firmly made,

Flashed out like glittering falchion blade.

Like thunder-bolts they moved the world,

And Tyrants from their thrones have hurled.

3

In seventeen hundred sixty-four,

I take you out to Warwick's shore,

They called it " Potowomot " then,

And liked the name—those sturdy men

There stood on edge ot sparkling stream

A Mill and Forge, with heavy beam ;

The wheel was driven by water-power,

To give the neighbors good rye flour,

The heavy fall of great trip-hammer

Sent through the trembling air its clamor,

While forging for the fishermen,

The bolts and anchors needed then.

Loud rings the anvil in the shop ;

We will not pass it by, but stop.

Within the compass of the hut

A vulcan stands, begrimed with smut,

Swings round his head the ponderous sledge,

And drops it on the fiery wedge,

Until, between the two, it shows

How much is done by vigorous blows.

Between the pauses of the heat

This youth ingenious made a seat, *

Where, waiting for his turn to strike,

He studied use of sword and pike,

Examined warlike movements, read

And stored them in his well-poised head.

This was Rhode Island's gifted son,

Who closely stood by Washington ;

In history his name is seen,

They call him, " brave Nathaniel Greene ! "

Of peaceful Friends his true extraction,

But more like warlike Knight, his action.

He put the British troops " to school "—

The Earl found him no Yankee fool.

In words of patriotic song—

Correct me if I quote it wrong—

" Cornwallis led a country dance,

" Much retrograde, and much advance,

---

* The old forge with his seat is well known to some of the present generation.

" The like thereof was never seen,

" His partner was Nathaniel Greene."

Through " Carolines " Greene's steps were bent

Like arrow from the bowstring sent,

Across Catawba, Yadkin, Dan,

In swift pursuit Cornwallis ran—

Their hands disjoined, away they whirl—

To old Virginia went the Earl,

Where Washington, his vis-a-vis,

Soon taught him how to bend the knee,

And there at Yorktown he did catch it,

George cut his plumes with his keen *hatchet*.

We 'll now dismiss the warlike theme,

And go where peaceful waters gleam.

Perchance our thoughts, while wandering there,

May drink in wisdom from the air ;

For who can live where waters roar,

And not increase his wisdom's store,

Or rest where peaceful wavelets reach
Along the quiet sandy beach,
And not accept the thoughts they teach ?

Below some rocks on Charlestown beach,
Almost as far as eye can reach,
Within the sweep of rolling surf.
And distant far from emerald turf,
Embedded deep in shifting sand
That fringes all that Township's land,
Are remnants of a noble ship,
Around whose ribs the algæ drip
In graceful streamers, each ebb tide,
Like Erin's banners flaunting wide ;
While gurgling through her timbers stout.
The briny sea goes in and out,
Hissing and spouting all day long,
In low, sad tones, a shipwreck song.

Beyond the reach of swelling tide,
And just below the green hill-side,

3*

In years gone by, an old house stood,

Its beams were made of white oak wood,

Where hard-wood pins with sharpened point

To hold more firmly morticed joint,

Were driven through the tenon's side

To keep such joints from opening wide ;

While at its end, outside, alone

A chimney stood, of gray-wacke stone,

To keep the mansion-house upright

Through heavy tempests, day or night.

Fixed in its top a stone of slate

Informed you of the builder's date.

The outside oven a child in 'teens

Might know was used for baking beans.

The heavy outer oaken door

Directly opened on the floor ;

No vestibule or " entry " there

Protected from the gusty air,

Yet summer's sun, or winter's rain,

Against its panels beat in vain.

Within, its cheerful owner sat;

Beneath his chair the purring cat;

In front, and glowing at his feet,

Was piled on high the burning peat.

Diffusing warmth about the room

And dissipating winter's gloom.

Each chimney corner held a boy,

His father's pride, his mother's joy;

And cuddling there, with flaxen curl

And azure eye, a laughing girl,

Reflection of the mother fair

Who sat in her creaking old arm-chair.

All through that day the murky skies,

Had taught a lesson to the wise,

And every dweller on that shore,

Had listened to the surge's roar;

Had seen with dread each hissing wave

High up the tiny sand-hills lave;

Observed the crested breakers foam

Far seaward with their snowy comb,

And dashing on with thundering shocks,
Break into spray on " Noyes' Rocks."

In leaden sky went down the sun,
Just as the tempest had begun,
And now came fiercely o'er the main
In dreadful gusts, the blinding rain.

Through darkness deep, lit up by spray,
That faintly showed the dangerous way,
Reeling before the dreadful gale,
Without the vestige of a sail,
A noble ship came driving fast,
Her voyage, finished, at last.

As avalanche from mountain height,
When moving with majestic might,
Takes up the crag amid the snow,
And hurls it thundering deep below—
So this doomed ship on crested wave
Was hurled resistless to her grave,

Striking the outer bar of sand,
A half mile distant from the land,
O'er which the breaking waves ran high,
And threw their billows to the sky.

Describe the scene that there occurred,
Repeat the prayers their Maker heard,
I cannot ; it would make you pale
Ere I recited half the tale :
Imagine it, all ye who can.
'T was never told by living man.
If any heard that dreadful crash,
They reckoned it the breakers' dash ;
If any heard that dying wail,
They thought it shrieking of the gale—
No intermission of the roar .
Of dashing rollers on the shore
Gave evidence beneath the waves
A score of men had found their graves.
. About the middle of the night
The tempest reached its utmost height,

But never failed that light to gleam,

Or from that friendly window stream,

Until the wind had died away

At ushering in the "break o' day,"·

When Deacon Wilcox sought his bed,

And laid to rest his nodding head.

Now while the household are asleep,

And Angels o'er them vigils keep,

Allow me to digress somewhat

And tell you of their daily lot—

Or rather, tell you of the " Deacon,"

Of all the country round, the beacon :

A leading man in Church and State,

A heart so kind it knew no hate,

A splendid man, a loving neighbor,

For whom the poor rejoiced to labor ;

Yet when he joined with you in trade,

He wanted *all* the profit made—

The trouble was his love of money,

He thought the hive was all *his* honey.

The Deacon knew his failing well,
Would often in church meetings tell,
With faltering voice and streaming eyes,
" He would above this sin arise."

The kind old man one night arose,
'T was just before the meeting's close :
He said, " he knew his carnal mind "
" To love of money was inclined,
" Resolved he was that very day,
" To travel in the better way,
" And to his great besetting sin,
" Henceforward never more give in ;
" If he had injured friends in trade,
" Fair restitution should be made,
" And if they'd state the sum in gold,
" The recompense should be fourfold."

A neighbor who was present there
Heard all his words, so seeming fair ;
He treasured up, and took in trust,
For future use, those words so just.

At early hour next day, he met
The Deacon, while the grass was wet.

With accents glad he shook his hand,
Rejoicing at the noble stand
So lately taken by his friend,
And wished the good resolve, no end.
He said, " he had a small affair,
" Which they would settle, then and there,
" Concerning that old brindled Ox,
" Who, cunning as a very fox,
" Would slip the yoke at every chance,
" And lead the boys a lively dance ;
" Or, fiercely plunging at the cow,
" Cause her to leave the old hay-mow ;
" It seemed as if the very de-vil,
" Possessed that brindled ox for evil.
" When bought, you said he was as kind,
" As any creature I could find,
" And represented him to be
" A pattern of humility.
" I paid you twenty dollars, gold,

" I do not wish it now fourfold,

" I only ask to have returned

" The money that was so hard earned :

" Give me the price, the Ox you take,

" And thus, ' fair restitution ' make."

These plain complaints the Deacon stirred,

For he remembered every word,   .

Knew them in substance to be true,

He scratched his head, " what should he do ? "

He thought the animal was sold,

For twenty dollars, British gold,

" And now he comes, that ugly beef,"

He wished him out far on the reef,

Beneath two fathoms of salt-water,

Or that he had been led to slaughter.

The friend had not much time to wait,

Before the answer came—'t was straight.

And while the words were firm, yet meek,

The argument was very weak,

4

His smile was sweet, his voice as clear
As any that we wish to hear.

" Dear Neighbor," thus the Deacon said,
With cheeks that slightly flushed with red ;
" No boys are we, but full grown men,
" Our years almost two score and ten,
" When we upon a trade agree,
" We never from its terms should flee ;
" Depend we must upon our eyes,
" Use our experience, shrewd and wise ;

" If we a losing bargain find,
" We should not be disturbed in mind,
" But cautious be, take greater care,
" Thereafter of that friend beware.
" The words you say you heard me speak
" Were spoken to sustain the weak
" Who falter in their daily walk,
" Those words, dear friend, were ' Meetin' ta

Like all the dwellers on the shore,

The Deacon did a wreck deplore,

With tenderness his heart o'erflowed

Toward those who on the billows rode ;

His house was e'er at their command,

To them he had an open hand,

His candle on tempestuous night

Became to them a beacon-light,

A refuge also, well they knew

Was offered there to shipwrecked crew—

But inconsistency again

In Deacon's character was plain ;

" Whatever comes from out the sea,"

He always said, " belongs to me " ;—

A godsend, was a stranded cargo,

On which his conscience laid embargo ; —

His golden rule was *thus* applied

To waifs upon the swelling tide : —

" The ownership by him is lost,

" Whose goods in ship are tempest-tost,

" The ownership in him remains,

" Who rescues them, and who regains."

The Deacon slept, while I 've told this

In form of a parenthesis,

And ere he wakes, return with me

To his old mansion by the sea.

The dreadful night at length had passed,

And cheerful daylight came at last —

Ah ! never will the night be o'er

To those who floated on the shore.

The gale had sensibly decreased,

The shrieking of the wind had ceased,

But still the scuds drove through the sky,

The thundering surges yet dashed high,

Though now to all 't was evident,

The storm its force had nearly spent.

What treasure-trove the Deacon gained,

That day before the sun had waned,

I never knew, I cannot tell,

He kept his business close and well.

But afterward his oak sideboard,

Had silver plate within it stored,

And oft deep in his spacious pocket,

A watch appeared, with golden locket ;

When asked if these were heirlooms old,

This story Deacon Wilcox told,

And when it was no longer new,

He might have thought it almost true.

" As I one day walked on the beach,

" The line of waves just out of reach,

" I heard a strange and curious noise,

" At first I thought it was my boys,

" Who imitate the call of birds,

" The grunting swine, the lowing herds,

" But looking closer at the matter,

" I saw it was a silver platter,

" Which, every time the waves did wash,

" Gave out the sound ' slop swash ! slop swash !' "
    4*

" Another day I walked along

" The sandy beach, and hummed a song,

" Heard something go, ' tick, whiz ! tick, whiz ! '

" Looked down and saw a watch-like phiz ;

" I snatched it from the moistened sand,

" And when I had it in my hand

" I saw a time-piece, quaint and old,

" Its face and cases, British gold.

" And well it was I came that way,

" It had been spoiled another day."

These stories of the watch and platter

Were always sure to end the matter,

The questioner, polite, receded—

He had the information needed.

Again went round the circling years,

Till eighteen hundred twelve appears ;

The blood upon the frozen snow

From patriot feet had ceased to flow,

And TRENTON was a joyful name,
To raise a patriotic flame.

Our Mother on the continent
A Treaty signed with us, at Ghent;
Yet, though she seemed quite mild and humble,
Continued still to growl and grumble,
So long the mistress of the sea,
She dreaded Yankee energy,
And soon a question grave arose,
That made us once again her foes.

The right our sailors to impress
She claimed as hers, without redress;
With sails aback, our ships must wait.
Until a boat could come " in state,"
And then select from out the crew
The strongest and the best in view,
While " Skippers " stood with hat in hand
With honied words and smile as bland,
Say "All is right," nor count it loss—
Such insults from St. George's Cross.

Mount Vernon's Chief lay with the dead,
To rest had Franklin laid his head,
But there were left some old-time teachers,
Who knew at glance, tyrannic features ;
They knew too well, their Country's flag
Was treated like a paltry rag ;
They saw that we must fight again,
Once more we must our rights maintain,
Or counted but as Britain's slaves,
Upon the land, and on the waves ;
They knew not then—our foes, so merry—
We had a JACKSON or a PERRY.

Amid the carnage, smoke and flame, (4)
With " hearts of oak," with loud acclaim,
Upon a beauteous western lake,
Our Country's flag I saw them take ;
And flaunting free in open boat,
From sinking ship defiant float ;
Within that fragile bark I saw
Resistance to tyrannic law,

And trembled lest the cannon's throat
Might shatter there the shallow boat.
With unbared head he stood upright—
The hero of that dreadful fight—
Until that flag from sinking wreck
Was hoisted o'er another deck,
And streaming out afar and wide,
Once more St. George's Cross defied.

What matter if I do not tell
The passing fight ; you know it well :
How 'mid the smoke, ere set of sun,
Our PERRY had the battle won ;
Had sent his famous war dispatch
That only once has had its match ;
It thrilled the heart of every land,
And reached to India's coral strand ;
Made strongholds of barbaric power
In Tunis and Algeria, cower ;
Its brevity so plainly stern,
Made tyrants from their courses turn :
Old Arrogance, of every nation,

Astounded, heard this short relation,

Divested of rhetoric flowers—

" *We've met the enemy; they are ours!* "

A few more words I wish to say

Before I close my roundelay,

To prove that from our native State

Her sons do not degenerate.

One instance only shall I quote,

The time you know, 't is not remote.

" Ball's Bluff " the selfsame story told

As when our Fathers fought, of old :

At first, 't was said with lying breath,

" Rhode Island men had fled from death,

" And left their guns without a strife

" Henceforth to live a coward-life."

Our little State was shocked, grew pale

While rumors whistled down the gale ;

But when that fatal field they sought,

When truth the lying rumor caught.

They found beneath the silent gun,
Rhode Island men who did not run.

Never again shall slander say
Of those brave men, *they ran away*;
Never again shall taunt of scorn
Be cast at men Rhode Island born !
But history this fact shall tell,
They bravely fought, they nobly fell ;
They *always* stood the battle shock,
Like firm, Rhode Island, Granite Rock !

＊＊●＊＊

My tales of olden times are told ;
Some, covered with the ages' mold
From sire to son are handed down,
With yet exceeding great renown ;
As thirsty earth the showers retain,
So these in youthful minds remain :
And if by true historic fact
You strictly measure every act,

These stories that we heard in youth
Would prove to be the words of truth.

Yet, if you to these scenes should go,
A contrast great the most would show,
The prints of feet in Kingstown rock,
Remain the curious sage to mock ;
The Charlestown beach, the surge's roar,
You find as in the days of yore ;
The mansion-house has given way
To fashion of a later day ;
The Deacon lies beneath the mound
Near yonder church, in sacred ground ;
Where once occurred the " Kingstown fight,"
A grassy meadow, green and bright ;
No more the warrior crouches there,
To shout infernal yells in air.

Where Williams shook the red man's hand
Behold a splendid City stand !
Whose institutions any State
Might well be proud to imitate ;

Tall spires her sloping hillsides crown,

Beside the classic halls of " Brown ":

The tramp and rush of busy feet

Resound throughout each well-paved street:

To savage yells that filled the skies

The locomotive now replies:

The whirling spindles give their hum,

Where once was heard the Indian drum;

Two hundred forty years to-day,

She 's stood resplendent on the bay;

Long may she stand on " What-cheer Rock."

Inhabited by Pilgrim stock,

Religious Freedom's firm defence,

Our noble City, PROVIDENCE !

5

NOTES.

An Icelandic historian, Torfæus, has claimed for his ancestors the glory of having discovered the New World. A learned work has also been published by the Royal Society of Northern Antiquaries, at Copenhagen, giving an account of the voyages made to America by the Scandinavian Northmen, during the tenth, eleventh, twelfth, thirteenth and fourteenth centuries. From this work, it appears that the ancient Northmen explored a great extent of the eastern coast of North America, repeatedly visited many places in Massachusetts and Rhode Island ; fought and traded with the natives, and attempted to establish colonies. One place which they called " Vinland " is supposed to have been Rhode Island. It is believed by Pro. C. C. Rafu and Finn Maguussen, that the celebrated inscripton on Dighton Rock was designed as an evidence of the occupancy of the country by the Northmen. It is similar to the " picture writing " of the Mexicans ; not to be read, but comprehended.

It was in the spring of 1636 that Roger Williams came over Seekonk river and settled at Providence, landing on "What Cheer Rock." The precise day of the month cannot be ascertained, but a letter was written by him from that settlement bearing the date, July 26th, 1636, O. S.

He was banished because he insisted upon unlimited toleration, or entire liberty of conscience, the sentence being passed by a council of Ministers and Magistrates, "as a disturber of the peace of the Church and Commonwealth." He named his "Plantation," "Providence"; "in a sense of God's merciful providence to him in his distress."

"The hardships and distress of the poor exiles who followed him, are hardly to be conceived by the present generation.

"He was the first person in modern Christendom to maintain the doctrine of religious liberty and unlimited toleration." [Callender.

The code of Rhode Island, as taken from its records, established in 1644, under the first charter from the Earl of Warwick, closes thus :

"All men may walk as their consciences persuade them, every one in the name of his God. And let the saints of the Most High walk in this Colony without molestation, in the name of Jehovah, their God, forever and forever."

(3.)

Upon a small island, in an immense swamp in South Kingstown, Rhode Island, Philip had fortified himself in a manner
superior to what was common among his countrymen. Here
he intended to pass the winter, with his friends. They had
erected about 500 Wigwams of a superior construction, in
which was deposited a great store of provisions. Baskets, or
tubs of corn, made of hollow trees, cut off about the length
of a barrel, were piled one upon another around the dwellings, to render them bullet proof. About 3000 persons had
taken up their winter residence there. The shape of the
island was similar to the shell of an oyster. The island was
surrounded by a ditch, or moat, containing water. It was on
the 19th of December, 1675, when the English marched up to
the fortress, and it was also the Sabbath day. The cold was
extreme, the air filled with snow, and it was one o'clock before
they arrived in the vicinity of the swamp. There was but
one point where it could be assailed with the least probability
of success, and that was fortified by a kind of blockhouse,
directly in front of the entrance, and had also flankers to
cover a cross fire. Besides high palisades, an immense hedge
of fallen trees, nearly a rod in thickness, surrounded it, encom-
passing an area of about five acres. Between the fort and
main land was a body of water, over which a great tree had
been felled, on which all must pass and repass, to and from
it. On coming to this place, the English soldiers, as many
as could pass upon the tree, which would not admit of two
abreast, rushed forward upon it, but were swept off in a
moment by the fire of Philip's men. Still, the English sol-

diers, led by their Captains, supplied the places of the slain.
Again and again were they swept from the fatal avenue.

Six Captains and a great many men had fallen, and a par-
tial but momentary recoil from the face of death took place.
Meanwhile a handful, under the fortunate *Moseley*, had, as mi-
raculous as it may seem, got within the fort at another place.

These were contending hand to hand with the Indians, and
at fearful odds, when the cry "They run ! they run !" brought
to their assistance a considerable body of their fellow soldiers,
and the slaughter of Indians became immense.

Flying from wigwam to wigwam, men, women and children
indiscriminately were hewn down, and lay in heaps upon the
snow.   Before the fight was over, many of the wigwams
were set on fire.   Into these, hundreds of innocent women
and children had crowded themselves, and perished in the
general conflagration.

Dr. Increase Mather said, in speaking of the fight :

" We have heard of two-and-twenty Indian Captains, slain
all of them, and brought down to hell in one day."

And in speaking of a Chief, he said : " A bullet took him in
the head, and dashed out his brains, sending his cursed soul
in a moment amongst the devils and blasphemers, in hell
forever."

(4.)

Perry was 27 years of age, when, on the 10th day of Sep-
tember, 1814, the British fleet sailed from Malden to attack
him. His squadron carried in all 54 guns ; the British
vessels, six in number, mounted 63 guns, *nine* more than

Perry's. On his own ship, the "Lawrence," after every gun but one was dismounted, and a large number of his own men killed, he saw the "Niagara," drifting out of the smoke of battle. Leaping into a boat, with his young brother, and standing erect at the helm with his flag flying from his boat, he ordered his men to "give way with a will." The enemy observed the movement, and directed their aim upon the boat. Oars were splintered in the rowers' hands by musket balls. and the men themselves covered with spray from the round shot and grape that smote the water on every side. Passing swiftly through the iron storm, he reached the "Niagara" in safety, and flung out his signal for close action. He bore down on the centre of the enemy's line, reserving his fire as he advanced, passing within close pistol range, through the hostile fleet, wrapped in flame as he swept on. Rounding to as he passed the line, he laid his vessel close to two of the enemy's ships, and poured in his rapid fire.

In fifteen minutes from the time the signal was made from the "Niagara's" spars, the battle was over. A white hand-kerchief waved from the "Queen Charlotte" announced the surrender. In his laconic account to the Secretary of the Navy, he used these words: "We have met the enemy, and they are ours!" Perry was a native of South Kingstown.